Naughty Girls Get Spanked

A collection of short stories of humiliation, BDSM, and the erotic touch only a Dom can provide

Claire Elliott

Table of Contents

Horny Birthday

Your 25th birthday present. Again I surprise you. You know nothing of the plans I have for you. All I have told you is that I have a nice hotel booked — a special surprise. You are curious about this time, but I do not tell you anything else. Your birthday falls on a Saturday, but we leave on Friday because your surprise is booked and I don't want to wait. What are we doing? You keep asking and guessing, but you are always wrong. You are so curious. I love your reaction every time I tell you that you are wrong. I decide to give you a hint, telling you that you will not need clothes, that other people are going to be involved, and that nothing that will happen what you "do not really want." I'm glad you don't know what it is yet.

First, we go to the hotel to check-in. I have booked the executive suite with an open bathroom, and I can see you taking a shower when I am in the room. I ask you to take a shower and tell you that I'll be back in a minute, then I'll leave the room for a while. I also asked you to put on a nice dress and to do yourself up before I left. I'll stay away for half an hour to give you time. I know you will be dancing in the shower and pampering yourself with the expensive lotions and shower gels I bought you as an early birthday gift. I hope you are thinking of the things I could do to make your heart beat faster and faster as you think of everything and fantasize about what tonight will have in store for you. About what could happen now that I leave you alone naked in the room, you are on your guard because, with me, you never know what will happen.

It is 3 pm when I arrive back at the suite, and I knock on the door, happy to see how beautiful you look as you open the door confidently. I smirk and walk passed you, going to the liquor cabinet and beginning to pour you a glass of red wine. You are beautiful, wearing a short black dress, sexy lingerie underneath, and black pumps. Your stunning smile and questioning eyes melt me as I ask you to sit. I can see you are still very suspicious because I behave a bit oddly. I see in your eyes that you are expecting something, but you really do not know what, and I am not solving anything for you either.

I will quickly take a shower while you watch and drink your wine. I put on a little show for you. I love that you laugh at the silly dancing that I am doing to your favorite songs, but your laugh quickly turns to you just biting your bottom lip as you see my dance turn sexual. I love that way you look at me as though I am the most fantastic thing that has ever happened to you. I get out and walk naked to the bed, where I have laid out my suit. I put it on, loving how well it fits. Drinking whiskey on the rocks, I wink at you as you finish your wine. I casually walk behind you and run my hand over your thighs and ass, reaching under your dress, my hand disappears to your wet pussy. I pull your thong to the side and push two fingers into your pussy without warning, filling you. Your ass begins to rock as you wriggle on my hand as I feel you reach behind you and unzip my trousers and watching as your hand disappears into my pants and pulls out my hard rod. You start to jerk me while I curl my fingers inside of you, feeling your pussy muscles begin to relax around the big intrusion. Your pussy begins to drip, and I pull out of you and push you onto your knees and hold your hair in a ponytail in my hand as I push my cock down your throat. I push down into you until your saliva is dripping from your mouth and onto my balls as my prick quivers down your throat, making me groan.

"Yeah, little bitch, let me use you like the slut that you are," I moan as I pump your mouth. Cumming, I smirk as I watch my cum spill from your mouth, making you gag. I let you struggle to swallow me before I push you flat on the bed and push your sexy dress up, push your knees back and expose your cunt to me. I love how you have no choice but to let me slide your pussy and your screams of pleasure only make my dick go harder as I trust into you. You come very quickly but I do not stop and hold you tightly by your ass now. I place a hand on your throat as I drill you, owning the pussy you have given to me. I release your throat, and my other hand glides over your breasts to your navel over your pussy to your thighs to grab your nice ass with both hands. I flip you over and pull your ass up and use my two thumbs to open your ass hole and start teasing you with my hard pole. Your ass is almost open, and you scream as you are taken hard. Without any effort, I let my dick slip into your ass while I hold on tightly to your ass. You will be cumming in a few seconds, but I will continue to take you until you fell limp, then I will also come in your nice ass.

By the time I am done with you, it is 6:30 pm, and we quickly fix ourselves up and head into the city. We go for a walk in the shopping streets and have a drink on a terrace. Time flies, and we go back to the hotel to have dinner, but we do not overeat. The drinks flow abundantly as we order a bottle of wine from the beautiful lady behind the bar. I can't take my eyes off you and take the half-drunk bottle of wine from our last order upstairs with us.

I open the door and immediately push your dress up again and start taking you from behind. I grope your tits and rip off your thong. I sit you down on the bed and begin pushing my cock into your tits as I paw at you. I love that you don't put up a fight. I pull your tits out of your dress and flick your nipples. I put your arms behind your back as I continue to push my hard cock onto you. Your huge tits feel like pillows next to my cock, and I groan as I begin to unzip my cock and let the pre-cum coat the tops of your tits. I move in front of you and push my cock between your huge tits, beginning to titty fuck you. I pull on your nipples and fuck your tits until I cum hard. You open your mouth as I have trained you, and I shoot my load over your tits and up into your mouth. Making you suck me off before I let you take a shower.

At 9 pm you will get half an hour from me to do what you want until 9.30 pm. You now put on a different dress — a blue one with a deep V neckline. You still have suspicions about what is about to happen, you don't trust it, and I won't tell you anything. 9.30 pm I have told you to expect anything that could happen to you. I know you are horny and still a little bit drunk, but now you have to wait a little while because I take you outside to the car.

After 5 minutes, I blindfold you and pull your dress up, exposing your pussy. When the car stops, you stay seated until I come to get you out after 10 minutes. I get you out of the car. You see nothing, and you have to trust me as we walk inside. It is nice and warm. You are blindfolded inside as well. Your coat is stripped off you. Your thong is also taken off. I carefully take off your blue dress until your bra is the only thing you are wearing. Now you are completely unsure of what is happening in a dark but cozy room where soft music plays. You can feel the warmth of the candles that burn.

I let you get a hold of me as your mind runs wild. You feel someone else's presence, and you hear rustling and suddenly the sound of high heels that are getting closer. There you are naked in a room that you cannot see. I hold my hand on your body, so you know I am beside you. Suddenly you feel strange hands between your breasts sliding down until your pussy, your ass, your legs your feet and back up. Suddenly you get a knock on your ass from those strange hands. You have long realized that it is a woman but do not understand the context. You will have to be patient. Now you are touched by the anonymous woman and me sensually.

"I will put you in nice fishnet stockings; I put a collar around your neck, I also put a leather strap around your right wrist and now on the left wrist. Do you still like it?" Asks the woman. You just nod as she now takes your hands and puts them on her head she lets your hands slide slowly over her body over her breasts to her belly over her ass and you crouch along to feel her legs and feet. She asks you to stay in this position and says how beautiful you are and what an ideal sub you are for her experiment. I see you now squatting with your legs open, giving me a nice view. I briefly explain how you can imagine the woman. She is blonde 5'8, C-cup. She has a beautiful but stern face. She is wearing a very short dress with high boots, her hair in a high ponytail. Now you know who you have in front of you even though you are not yet allowed to look. You now also know where you are I think. Okay, you say. I found this stunning woman on the internet; she is a BDSM Mistress and was looking for a sub who equaled her style.

You are now squatting there, and she asks you to "stick your tongue out of your mouth," and she brings her pussy to your tongue and orders you to slowly lick her pussy. She asks, do you like it? Yes, you answer, you have to stand up, and she tells again.

"I am going to put a strap around your ankles," piece by piece, she asks if you would like your dear husband to do that while she looks and commands. She tells me first to do the right ankle but very sensual. I rub your thigh down very slowly over your knee your leg to your ankle while I lick your wet pussy I put the strap around your wet pussy, it is a message for me that you like your surprise.

"Now the left, but you have to stand behind her," she says. I now take your ass and let my two hands roam over your left ass and thigh, slowly going down and licking your ass while I put on the strap. She now takes you to a 2nd room that is a furnished BDSM room with a chair, a crossbar, and a doctor's bench. You will have to use your imagination now. She ties you to the crossbar with arms and legs spread. Once she has you secured, a whip and a vibration on your pussy makes you cry out in bliss. Out of nowhere, you feel my hard pole disappearing backward into your pussy while you heavenly crumble with the vibration on your clit. The woman fucked you gently and licks your breasts. Nipple clamps are fastened to your full breasts, and I enjoy you cumming after having literally only had to fuck you for a few minutes. She ties you in a chair with leg supports; she rubs your pussy and your ass with lubricant. She lubes the strap on dildo and puts it in your pussy as I hug and caress you everywhere. Unfortunately, you can not do much to fight us off because you are tied up, and another orgasm is forced upon you.

She doesn't give you time to recover from your orgasm as she unties you and drags you over to the doctor's table. She lays you down as cum is still dripping from your cunt, and she opens your legs. She orders you to open your mouth, and she takes my cock tight. She pulls it gently while she kisses your tongue. She pulls me closer to my own orgasm. She sucks my dick for a moment, and she takes my dick and puts it in your mouth. She pushes my ass to push it harder down your throat. She now lets me continue quietly. Suddenly you feel a wet tongue on your pussy. She finds you so sexy that she wanted to eat you. Now she wants to see how I take you and loosens your hands your blindfold a little looser, not so much that you can see clearly though. I start to take you slowly in your wet pussy. She comes to your mouth with her now wet pussy. You eat her now and touch her. She comes quickly, ready to feel your hands all over her body. She rips off your blindfold, and now you can see her. She gives your eyes time to recover, and soon I see a pleasant look in your eyes. She began to take off her strap-on and now talks a little with you about how you liked it. You express how much you liked it, and she asks if you want to continue. You nod your head excitedly, and I am so happy that you like your birthday present.

"Okay, we will get something to drink and have a rest," she explains.

After 20 minutes, you are on the crossbar again

with your legs tied up. You are now in a squat position. She licks your pussy and strokes your ass, she pushes two fingers in your pussy and gives me the sign to stand behind you with her other hand she takes my now hard dick and sticks it in your ass. I take you now in a way that we have never tried before. You scream in pleasure while she fingers your pussy. It is now dark, only a very dull red candle still burns. She moves so she is now also standing behind you and pulling on your hair until you head bends towards the mirrored ceiling while I take you hard. You feel a breath on your chest you want to look, but you can't because she pulls your head backward, keeping you secured. You feel a body gently press against your front where a hard dick disappears in your pussy. A man takes your breasts in his hands and takes your pussy while I take your ass. You let it all happen while you look into my eyes from my shoulder you kiss me and further enjoy your long-awaited fantasy; the man fucks you in a sensual way like you're used to from me. I also like to see you, so enjoy them as I let your hair go now. You can look at him, where he kisses you on your neck. You come hard as you kiss him back on his neck. To which he cums, I push a little further in your nice ass and come then also. The man discreetly disappears. We get you loose now you can rest for a little while you hear my conversation with the woman who said that the man was her husband and we get dressed again. We go back to the hotel. In the hotel, I tell you in the shower how exciting and sexual you are and how I greatly enjoyed watching what the 2nd man and the woman did to you.

The Rugby Team

I stood there then. A spreader bar kept my feet apart, ballgag in my mouth, anal hook in my butt that was connected by a chain to my handcuffed hands behind my neck and, of course, a blindfold and collar. I felt the warmth of spotlights on my body. But how did I end up here?

Let me introduce myself first. I am Jasmine, a married woman of 42 years. In my previous marriage, I had two children, and that meant that my body was no longer as tight as I would like. I was, as men would say, a woman with a comfortable body. I have wide hips, long, slightly curly brown hair, and E-cup breasts with piercings through both nipples. After my previous relationship went wrong, I met my current husband, Ryan. We have a wonderful relationship, and I have my children every other week, so that gives me a lot of freedom.

Gradually, I discovered that my new husband had experimented a lot in the past with sex. That stimulated my curiosity considerably because I had only very little experience. During a game of sex after an evening with a lot of wine he suddenly gave me a big slap on my ass, it was as if an electric shock went through my body and of sheer horniness and wild lust. I shouted to him that he would agree this slut had to fuck well. After this sex party, we started talking, and it turned out that his experiments had been mainly in the field of BDSM. He told me his experiences, and it turned out that he was very fond of submissive women. I wanted to know everything. The whole conversation excited me enormously, and my husband did not miss that either. Suddenly he said with a stern look and voice, "On your back, legs wide and finger yourself ready for me slut." I had not expected this turn for a moment. I obeyed quickly, turned on my back, and spread, with some embarrassment, my legs, and started playing with my pretty wet cunt. He took a good seat in front of me and ordered me to cum only after his permission. I was so far gone that I no longer responded to his command, and he immediately showed what would happen if I didn't. He grabbed both my nipples and squeezed them viciously.

"If I tell you something, you respond with, yes, master," he growled.

"Yes, master," I said with difficulty. Good slut, was his reaction while he let go of my nipples. Go on, he said, and I concentrated on my horniness again.

Soon an orgasm presented itself, and my husband, who could see my body wriggling, reminded me that I could only come after his permission. That was not that easy, but after his final permission, I experienced an unusually explosive orgasm. This was my first experience with BDSM. This dynamic continued and evolved to the point where we had arrived. We do not have a 24/7 D / S relationship, but we do approach that. I am his fully subservient slave, and within the limits that we had agreed, he can do whatever he wants with me. One of the hard limits agreed at the beginning was that no one other than the two of us was involved in our game. Some time ago, I confessed to him that I sometimes had fantasies of being sold as a slave to the highest bidder. He indicated that he had difficulty with this, especially the sharing of his great love was against him, but he was not unwilling about it. Furthermore, we had not really talked about this until this morning with coffee. He spoke to me and reminded me of my fantasy and told me that it was going to come true that same evening.

I was instructed to be ready in the usual outfit at 1800 hours. During the day I was quite nervous! Finally, it was 1800 hours, and I was ready as desired. Pumps, a leather collar, and a long jacket, that was all.

After having driven for a while, we arrived at a remote but very spacious house. Before we stopped, he handed me a blindfold that I had to put on. After he let me get out of the car, I was led somewhere, which turned out to be a front door that was opened immediately.

I heard a man's voice say to my husband, "Is this the thing for tonight?" I heard Ryan say that it was, and I was led inside. Once inside, someone clicked something on my collar, and I was led further into the house. We arrived in a room, and Ryan took off my coat, and I was naked. He kissed me passionately and whispered, "Good luck, slut" in my ear and walked away. Shortly after that, someone else entered the room, who gave me a nasty flick on my nipple and followed with the command "bend over bitch." I responded immediately and did what I was told. I felt that something was running cold between my buttocks, and I quickly realized that it had to be lubricant because I quickly felt something cold penetrate into my ass. I immediately felt the cold metal against my wrists and felt that something went around that clicked shut, so handcuffs. I felt that the thing in my ass was pulled uptight and my hands down. Suddenly I felt a stabbing pain in my nipples, and I was instructed to open my mouth that was immediately filled by a round rubber ball. I felt that a strap was fastened behind my head and the ballgag was in place.

After another tap on my buttocks, I was summoned to follow, and I was carefully led away by the strap of my collar and finally into a warm room from which a loud buzz was heard. In the warm room, I walked three steps and then stopped. Someone gave a sensitive tap to my nipples and ordered that I had to spread my legs on which I felt something close to both my ankles, and I noticed that I could no longer close my legs.

The murmur fell silent, and someone began to speak. "Dear friends," he said, "we are again here today to auction some slaves, and I have admired the merchandise and must say that excellent merchandise has been offered again." Goddamn, I was starting to get really nervous; there was really no way back! I really want this shot through my head, but my already wet cunt already answered.

The speaking master stated that the auction could start and announced the first merchandise. Ladies and gentlemen, the first slave girl to be auctioned, is the exotic beauty, Trisha. Pussy, it wasn't my turn yet, so more time for nerves. Bidding starts with 10 dollars, who offers more? Soon the bids rose to 100 dollars, and eventually, they hammered out at 130 dollars.

The auctioneer kept up the pace and went on, and the next slave girl is the thick beauty Jasmine! A shock goes through my body when I realize that the moment has really arrived, it is now my turn! I am directed forward and notice that I am turning slowly; probably, I am standing on some rotating platform so that everyone has an excellent view of my body.

The bids start again at 10 dollars, but at 90 dollars, there is no new offer. Disappointed, I realize that I am really worth more than a meager 90 dollars. Just at the moment that I am giving up hope for a better offer, a new voice sounds powerful for me that offer 180 dollars. The auctioneer responded with surprise and repeated that the previous bid was at 90 dollars. The bid's voice answers cryptically that he is also not bidding for him alone. Since nobody makes a bid against it, the auction master is hammering at 180 dollars. Someone removes my spreader bar, and I am led down the stairs on my leash and notice that I am being transferred to my new owner.

My heart is pounding in my throat! What will happen to me? Where am I going, who are they? But despite my nerves and tension, I notice that the whole event does not leave me untouched, I feel the wetness between my legs!

I am being carried on my leash, and I expect that

we will go outside, but before I feel the outside air, I feel a jerk on the chain, and I stop.

"Kneel, bitch." I hear to which I naturally respond immediately. I notice that several people enter the room, and the same voice continues with a slightly louder voice, "see our bitch here and use her for what she was purchased for!" I am pulled up by my nipples, and my handcuffs and anal hook are removed. I hear "bend over slut," and I feel a rod at my waist that I bend over and my shoulders touch metal too. My wrists are fixed, and my legs are played with a spreader bar. I immediately feel a cock against my lips that immediately slides into my mouth. At a slow pace, I am pounded in my throat, deeper and deeper, until I feel his balls hit my chin with every stroke. I feel hands exploring my body everywhere.

"What udders that slut has" I hear someone say while my nipples are pulled roughly, then I feel a stabbing pain in my nipples when someone puts nipple clamps on it. Another hand explored my ass and felt between my legs.

"Omg, that bitch is soaking wet," I hear someone say.

"What a horny slut," another voice says. A big cock is pushed into my wet slit that immediately starts to fuck me. At the same time, my ass cheeks are whipped in the same rhythm as the banging cock in my pussy. This one stops for a moment, and I feel something against my ass, this is being gently stretched by more and more fingers that are later replaced by a very big butt plug, Jesus, it seems as if my anus is torn. But the gentlemen do not care. My cunt and mouth are ruthlessly fucked. I hear the guy who fucks my throat moan.

"I'm going to squirt in that slut's mouth," and before he is finished, I can feel his cock getting harder, and waves of hot cream are sprayed down my throat. I try to swallow everything away, but that doesn't work, and I feel it running down my chin. His cock is pulling back, but its place is immediately taken by another who is a bit thinner but a lot longer. This cock knows no mercy and immediately rammed it into my mouth. I can hardly suppress my gag reaction.

Meanwhile, the cock in my cunt is also getting ready to cum. His cream runs down my legs. Because of his fierce thrusts, my tits swing back and forth to the rhythm of his pumps, and the person who works my ass with a whip is also in rhythm.

Goddamn, I'm used like a slut with three cocks in my holes. This realization only makes me hornier than I already was. I felt the cock using my throat come, and I get a second load of hot juice to swallow, which I cannot quite manage. The shaft that my cunt just filled up with, pulled back, and the person who just worked the whip on my ass stops. My wrists and ankles are released. Someone pulls me up by my hair and directs me roughly a few steps away. Clamps on my nipples are pulled as I am pulled down with the words "kneel bitch." Apparently, I am over someone directing his pole into my cunt. My hair is pulled forward so that another pole can be rammed into my mouth. At the same time, the butt plug is taken out of my ass, and I hear someone say, "So, let's see if the bitch's ass is ready." I think this is going to be hot. I have never been taken in my cunt and ass at the same time. But the men again prove that I am just a set of fuck holes because, without pardon, a big greased pole slides into my ass. I can only groan because of the cock in my throat. It seems as if the gentlemen are only steaming up now, I feel a popping orgasm appearing to come from the depths of my being, and I come groaning and shaking while I am still mercilessly fucked in my holes. Once one cock is finished, the next one takes its place.

This goes on for a while; I have no idea of how many cocks have already been put into my body, but my jaws are getting stiff, and my ass and pussy are on fire. The last cocks are pulled back, and the hair of the underlying guy pulls me. Again I am put on my knees but now follow the command "finger yourself bitch." Obediently, I start fingering my slit that is wet with multiple creampies and my own juices. I notice that there are people around me, and I hear that they are jerking themselves off.

"Time for the grand finale," someone says. One by one, I feel blobs of cream everywhere on my body while I come again hard. When no one comes out anymore, I am told that I have to clean every cock. One after the other, my mouth is used, and I lick and suck each cock completely clean.

Then I hear the voice that also commanded me to say that they had to deliver me as they had received me. I am led somewhere and hear water running. I am put under a shower, completely soaked and dried. The ballgag and anal hook are put back (which is very easy now), and I am led away on the leash under loud applaud. Suddenly I notice that the temperature in the room where we come changes.

"Here is your slave again, exactly as we

promised," I hear someone say. Thank you, man, I suddenly hear Ryan's famous voice say. Did you use her well, he asks. "Sure," the stranger says, "My God, what a well-trained horny bitch you own," he says after it. I'm proud of my slave-girl, Ryan says while he puts on my coat and leads away on the leash and helps me get into the car. There he removed the blindfold, and I look around in surprise and at Ryan's smiling face.

"Was it a nice baby?" He asks while he takes his phone and shows me something. There I sit on the small screen, kneeling between 11 stiff cocks and 1 in my mouth.

"Amazing, I have finished a whole football team!" I said, looking at the cocks.

"Rugby team, he said, laughing while we drive away, and I fall into a blissful sleep.

Horny Weekend

She hailed a taxi and quickly got in. She knew she was hot. She knew she was horny. Despite the air conditioning, it was warm in the back of the car. But she would have preferred it to be even warmer. She glanced up from her phone to her bare legs and imagined that the man she had been sexting let his warm hands glide up her thighs to the edge of her thong. Then she would spread her legs and be toyed and groped by him. She looked up from her phone. She put it face down on her thigh and looked out the window. She knew she was blushing and didn't want the taxi driver to get the wrong idea. She wasn't blushing for him.

She had planned a family vacation without sex. At least, without sex with others. She had packed her beloved toys, though she did not know if she would have enough privacy to use them. The man on the other end of her phone intrigued her even though he was a lot older than she was. Despite this, the photos she had seen of him were not disappointing. Compared to the guys she had dated in the past, he was by far the most handsome man she had ever entertained. For a moment she closed her eyes and imagined she was coming into the hotel room and he was in her bed. She wouldn't kick him out. He had managed to get a place in her young head in a strange way, the intoxicating type. The kind of frenzy that made heartbreak last for years.

She looked down at her thigh and fought the urge to open it and read the message she just felt come through. She knew she was only a short distance to the hotel and smiling to herself and shaking her head, she opened the phone again. She smiled as she read the filthy message he had written, tightening her pussy as her clit throbbed.

When she arrived at the hotel, she was happy that there was still enough time to swim in the hotel's pool. She took a refreshing dip in the water and imagined that he was looking at her from the other side of the pool. Then she would swim towards him and hang on the edge where he stood. She would look up at his body and feel how he admired her because although she had shown little of herself, she did not doubt that he would like her. Just like how the two boys, her age playing with a ball in the water, looked at her. She swam to the edge. She felt her swimsuit thong hold their gaze as she slowly made her way out of the water, dripping water to the floor. It excited her, just as it excited her that her nipples were visible behind the thin yellow bikini as she walked to the sauna. It seemed deserted. She took off her still wet bikini and looked at her naked body. Her nipples were half stiff, with the exciting feeling that she had been feeling for the last few hours. For a moment, she stroked her thighs, stopping only as her fingers reached her pussy. She knew she was wet. If anyone had entered the sauna, she would not have minded. But ten minutes passed silently. Deciding that she needed to leave, she reluctantly put her bikini back on and left the sauna, deciding that she should head to the restaurant.

The restaurant was chic — almost too chic for the dress she was wearing as she had come straight from the pool and sauna. She had regularly received messages from him and further provided him with a few photos that made clear what she was doing. She had decided it was a good idea to keep him informed. As she began to start her meal, she choked.

"That's not possible. Is it him?" She thought as she coughed. A man his age entered the hotel restaurant. He was smartly dressed in black trousers and a white shirt, which fitted him better in the atmosphere of the restaurant than most other guests, some of whom were dressed in shorts. He sat down alone at a table, no more than 5 meters away, with his face toward her. She picked up her phone. No message, at least not from him. For a moment, she considered sending him a message. But that could seem too intrusive. If it

was him, if he had come here for her, she would have to wait. He drank white wine and only ate a starter. The main course and dessert could not go fast enough. If he got up, she'd have to follow him. Because although he did not contact her in any way, she never doubted it for a moment. It was him.

"I'm going for a swim," she said loudly to her family members as they came into the restaurant. She hoped that he would hear it and follow her to the pool. While her family members remained seated, she ran to her room, wrapped the towel around her slender hips, and ran to the pool.

The pool area was dark and sensual, and she was happy that no one else was swimming there. The sign said it would be open for another hour. She hoped he would come to the pool, but saw no one. Just when she wanted to put her towel and phone on a chair, her phone vibrated — a message from him.

"Undress. Swimming in your bikini is not

necessary." Her heart skipped. His message clearly left no room for discussion. She knew she was going to obey. She looked around again. The pool was completely deserted. Maybe he was outside? She did what he had asked and quickly jumped into the water. It was clearly colder than a few hours ago as if the heating had already stopped pending the closing time. She came up and shook the water from her long hair. A man stood at the edge of the pool. Black pants, white blouse.

"Come here, you," he said softly. As she swam to his side, he took two steps back. She lingered on the edge of the water. She would have preferred to look up. She didn't dare. She did not know if it was allowed.

"Come out of the water," he said. She obeyed him and crawled on the edge of the pool. She stayed on her knees so that he could see her back and the upper part of her ass well. She threw her right arm in front of her breasts, out of an exciting shame.

"Just stand up." Again she obeyed. She

covered her waist with her left arm. But she felt naked. Wonderfully naked.

"You can lower your arms." First, she lowered her left hand. She felt his gaze on her horny cunt, getting wetter and more excited every second. He stretched out his hand and touched her clit. She closed her eyes with desire, but he withdrew his hand almost immediately.

"Put that other arm away too." She put both her hands on her back, proud of the nakedness she was allowed to show him. He took a black cloth from his pocket.

"Turn around." She obeyed, felt that he was taking a step forward and saw it getting dark. She was blindfolded.

"You don't ask questions. But if you say no, I will stop."

"Yes, sir," she answered. After the blindfold was tied tightly, she felt how he tied ropes around her wrists. He then pulled her hands up. It didn't hurt; on the contrary, it felt nice. It seemed like art how he tied her hands to her back. She could no longer move them, and yet it was comfortable. Finally, he put a band around her neck. For a moment, she was afraid that he would tighten it, but he let it hang fairly loose.

"We will walk to my room in a minute. I cannot promise that no one will see you." She was shocked. The idea excited her, but there was also the fear that one of her family members would see her like this. She would not know what to do. But she said nothing.

"Here." She felt how he put her towel around her shoulder. For a moment, she hoped he would wrap the towel around her, but it was clear that her shoulder was only for the towel. She did not wear a towel to cover her nakedness. For a moment, she considered asking him if he would like to take her bikini with her. But she knew that was a pointless question. He gently pulled the chain attached to her collar.

"We are going to go for a walk." He led her through the hotel, warning of every step, and every stair. And with every step she took, the confidence grew. She heard no one, not even when they stepped into the elevator. She heard him swipe the key card over the door and felt the cold air harden her nipples.

"After you." For a moment, his hand stroked her naked ass. He pushed her in, step by step. The room was clearly larger than hers because it seemed to take forever for him to stop her.

"You are now in front of the bed. Carefully get in — on your knees." He gently pushed her into the right position.

"There you go," he said. His hands stroked the inside of her thighs and pushed her legs a little further apart. Slowly his fingers began to play with her cunt while she was defenseless on her knees. Defenseless and horny. While his right index finger slid into her and slowly began to spoil her, he bent his head to her ear.

"I am here like you for a long weekend. I'm here for you as long as you want me," he said, sending chills down her spine.

"I am going to enjoy this," he said as she felt

him pull his hard cock from his pants and pierce her cunt without warning. He hardly had to force himself inside as her wet pussy let him in easily. He held her hips and humped her aggressively, making her gasp as she felt his cream suddenly pour into her. It had been nice, but not nearly as intense as she had hoped. He pulled out, wiped the blindfold off, and untied her hands. He handed her her bikini and towel and told her to go to her own room. She walked out, confused, hoping for more instructions, but they didn't come. She walked back to her room and wondered what had just happened. Had she done something wrong? Had she been disappointing to him? Was she perhaps too young?

She walked into her room and sat blankly on her bed. Next to her was the lingerie she had packed. She reached out and stroked the fabric from the two sets she had brought with her. One virgin white, the other one, crimson lace with black detail. She checked her phone, still no message from him, not a single sign. She went to the bathroom and fitted both sets, trying to kill some time while she processed her disappointment. He had not satisfied her hunger, only teased her, and then taken her pleasure away.

"Maybe I should get mad at him," she thought to herself.

"That he just abandoned me. That he starts and doesn't finish." She looked at her phone hoping that he had sent her a message

If he has sent a message, I will not reply, she thought. For a moment, she considered messaging herself. She restrained herself.

"Be at the gate of the parking lot in five minutes," the message read. She was shocked.

"What are we going to do then?" She replied. She knew it wasn't supposed to ask, but she didn't need long to decide to do it anyway. She trusted him despite everything, but she didn't know him well enough. And he had to do something to win her trust.

"We are going to give you a great night," she was sent back immediately. She laughed for a moment.

"I want that," she replied, then quickly pulled her black dress out of the suitcase, went to the bathroom, brushed her teeth for half a minute, and tried in the short time she had to bring her hair into decency. She put on her black high heels, grabbed her purse and phone and hurried outside.

"Damn it," she thought as the door closed behind her.

The room key, she thought. But there was no time left to think about it.

Although dusk had fallen, she saw him standing at the gate that separated the castle hotel and parking lot from the outside world. He was casual, dressed in black and white. As if he wasn't waiting for anything. She felt better and walked over to him. She stopped a meter away and looked him in the eye. A small smile came to his mouth. A friendly smile. Friendly and at the same time compelling.

"Come here," he said. She took a half step

forward, her heart thumping in her throat. He did not move his lower body, only extended his hand — just enough to touch her dress. She looked him in the eye as she felt him pull it up. A sultry summer wind stroked her thighs.

"Beautiful," he said, pulling her to him. In an instant, she was trapped. His hand clutched her buttocks. He pressed her mouth to his and opened her lips with his tongue. His tongue played for a moment. A delicious tingling flowed through her body. This was no more kissing; this was ecstasy. She felt her newly purchased panties get wet, pressing her lower body against his thigh. She didn't have to wait long. She felt his fingers over the edge of her thong. Moaning, she let them come inside. Shockingly, her hips indicated the rhythm he had to play. He played it. He kept kissing her while he played. She tasted his tongue, his mouth. It tasted better than in her wildest dreams.

"Let go," he whispered in her ear. She obeyed. In the background, she heard a car pass by.

Further away was the sound of people sitting on the patio caught her attention. She heard it, but it was as if the sounds were not there. What she really heard was the sound of his fingers, letting her own moisture flow down her thighs. After she had finished, he sat down half on his knees in front of her. With his tongue, he wiped her moisture from her thighs from her pussy. He pulled her thong further down until it hung on her ankles. She could no longer walk in a normal way. But she still felt she had to let it go. A car stopped. He turned her around with a quick gesture, and in the same movement, she was taken away. A blindfold covered her eyes. She felt how he pushed up her dress. The wind flowed through her naked pussy. The door of the car opened.

"Get in," he ordered. She didn't even have to obey. She felt pushed into the car like a handcuffed criminal, her head protected by his hand resting on her. To her reassurance, he took a seat next to her. She expected that he would give the driver a clue, but without saying a word, the car drove away. And before it was up to speed, she suddenly felt his mouth nestle in her crotch. She spread her legs slightly so that his tongue could penetrate deeper into her. He tasted her clit, penetrated her with his tongue. She would have liked nothing better than to be able to stroke his penis, feeling his hard cock against her mouth. But she knew she had to wait.

Like-Minded

My name is Tammy, and I like to explore my sexual boundaries and lusts. This story is about Jordan, my "kryptonite," so to speak, something you want, but you already know it will never work.

Everyone with a tinder account recognizes the moment, I think. It feels like you have been swiping for an eternity, but that perfect match is not forthcoming. As time goes on, you may be more likely to settle for someone who was swept to the left at the start of your swipe session, but you think out of sheer frustration and lack of attention; they will do. This also happened to me. I, a 26-year-old woman, saw this 29-year-old man pass by on Tinder and thought, he'll do. Not because the man in question, is unattractive, but more simply not my type at all. The typical metroman, with a hip haircut, his so-called own clothing label, DJ as a full-time job, and his popular social media accounts, also show him to be the popular joke maker. I, an old-fashioned soul who would rather have all her music on LP and dance barefoot between my antique things while smoking a joint, would have laughed half a year ago if someone had told me that a typical DJ metro man was a lust object for me. And even a safe haven — an unmistakable click between two people with completely different lives, but who are likeminded.

I found him terrible at; first; he was fronting so hard online, but I decided to chat back to him. He reacted at lightning speed every time. The typical type of pretty boy who was on his phone all day to see if he still got likes on his social media profiles, that's how I saw him. In no time at all, he started to ask about my sexual wishes, which I would, in principle, have no problems with if I had felt attracted to him. Although I could not deny that something in his answers intrigued me, I wondered when he would finally leave me alone, I reacted less and shorter, but this proved not to affect him whatsoever. I decided to completely ignore him for a few days, hoping that this would be forever.

A few days later, I felt bored again; I have always been a girl of peaks and troughs and can sometimes experience my emotions in a somewhat extreme way. Loneliness is a recurring emotion and an emotion that I never talk about easily with anyone. I wanted a listening ear or shoulder to cry on but could not find it. In recent years, I have become the queen of socially isolating myself. At that moment, Jordan appeased me again, and I could no longer ignore him. For some reason, I poured out my heart to him, about how over-emotional I can be and how I have the feeling of being a burden to everyone, how alone I sometimes feel when I often choose to be open and vulnerable, how scared I actually am sometimes of people. He listened with angelic patience and heard everything I wanted to share at that moment. He admitted that he recognized himself in me, but that he often kept that part of himself to himself. At that moment, I met Jordan from a completely different side, and suddenly, there was no turning back. I exposed myself emotionally to him and him to me; we turned out to be much more alike than we had initially thought. I became so curious about him; everything suddenly changed after that conversation. We talk about our ways of being and how this sometimes made our lives a lot more complicated than they needed to be. I found peace with him; he did not judge me and was always willing to listen to me and did this in the most pleasant way for me.

From that moment on, I was suddenly able to open myself up sexually for him even though I would never have turned around for him on the street. We also found a lot in common in the sexual area.

A relationship doomed to fail because of the

different lives we led but too curious about each other to stop it. I was in my final semester of college, and I didn't want to meet Jordan until I graduated, I was far too afraid that from the first meeting he would be sitting in my head 24/7. For two months, we chatted over apps to each other every day, supported each other everywhere, and shared our sexual fantasies with text, photos, and videos.

I cannot deny that he started to excite me terribly for someone who is not my type in appearance. There was no filter on this man, and he didn't try to hide his desires from me, I enjoyed it intensely. He sometimes drove me crazy; I woke up in the morning with videos he had made for me at night. These videos went from simply jerking himself off and spraying his cum over printed out photos of me to showering sensually for me, music playing in the background, and him dancing for me. Because of the dirty images that we exchanged, he was constantly in the back of my mind, and every morning when I got up to work on my thesis, I first had to play with myself so that I could focus somewhat on my graduation research. But even then, he and his slightly small but beautiful penis shot through my head every few minutes, making me crave it.

I wanted to know how he moaned, how his hard cock would feel in my wet pussy; I wanted to know how his cum tasted. I wanted it everywhere, in my face, over my tits, in my pussy. When I thought of Jordan, it sometimes seemed as if my pussy had a heart that could actually beat. I couldn't wait to see him. We are both the type of people who tend to treat the other like a toy and when in a relationship, not to take it seriously.

When did finally agreed to meet up, a week before my degree was over, we agreed to meet at my place. The bell rang, and a dash of panic shot through my body. I sneaked softly to the door and checked myself in the mirror. I stood on my toes to see if it really was Jordan through the eye of the door. It really was him. I opened the door, and Jordan immediately took a step in my direction and gave me three quick kisses on my cheek, I was actually about to sucker punch him for trying his moves on me but just let him, I liked that he was obviously nervous. I walked into the corridor with him and was amazed at how much I was attracted to his appearance. We stopped walking halfway down the corridor, there was no reason for it, but we decided to both lean against the wall and looked at each other again. We laughed a little uncomfortably; he looked at me with a fascinated look that made me feel a bit insecure.

"So, do I look like my photos?" I heard myself asking.

"No, really not at all," he answered.

"What? Are you serious?" I said I was shocked and slightly offended.

"Yes, you look totally different. I like the real-life version a lot more," he replied, teasing me with his cheeky smile. At that moment I got so stuffy that I just didn't know where to look. I literally broke out in a sweat.

"So you find me uglier than on my photos or what? I have never heard this before." I hear myself saying in a defensive tone and still hoping that I will stop talking, but it turned out that I needed an answer.

"Not necessarily uglier or smarter, but simply different." Jordan seemed entertained. I felt that the tension that started to run from all pores of my body gave him a kind of confidence boost. He had the most relaxed attitude I had ever seen with a man on a first date; he even suggested that we grab a beer from my fridge after a few minutes when he was inside — my fridge. I walked to the kitchen and grabbed two beers before going back to the couch and sitting down awkwardly. By coincidence we reach for the same beers at the same time on the table in front of us, we look at each other, and suddenly we are stuck to each other's faces. Thank fucking God, it happened. We kissed each other surprisingly soft but passionate, his lips felt soft, and his tongue was careful and sweet against mine. But soon, his hands found a way to my breasts. A playful romp followed, and he tried to slip his hands under my shirt, and I tried to dodge his hands but secretly teased him with mine. He did not give up, and I decided to take charge; I sat on top of him and pressed myself completely against him. I felt through my clothes how my clit rubbed his hard cock that was neatly hidden in his pants, and I couldn't resist it, I had to ride it. Our sweet kiss turned into a dirty and horny tongue session. Jordan grabbed my face with one hand and squeezed my mouth open. Without hesitation, he spat into my mouth and closed my mouth again, making me swallow his spit. I looked at him with my eyes, asking for his cock, and he knew exactly what my gaze meant. I saw that twinkle in his eyes, and meanwhile, I felt how he pushed his dick harder against me and held me tightly. We kissed so wetly that half of our faces were covered in spit, but it didn't matter, that was part of the fun. After a while, we decided it was really time for Jordan to go; it was a bit too much for both of us; we wanted each other so badly. Terribly frustrated and horny, I shuffled to the door of my living room to bring him to the front door and let him out, but halfway down the corridor, I decided to curl my back and stick my ass out to him.

"Spank my butt as hard as you can," I said, looking at him from over my shoulder. Jordan didn't hesitate for another second and gave me three hard blows on my ass.

"That's what you need, isn't it?" He growled, making my clit throb even more. I smile with him and walk towards the front door again, but suddenly I am pushed with full force towards the front door, and I feel my whole body crashing against it. As if lightning went through my whole body, not with fright or pain, but pure horniness. I like this. Jordan came up against me while I was still standing with my body pressed against the door, he pressed his stiff cock (neatly in his pants) against my buttocks while I no longer had any control over my body and I willingly accepted him as he dry humped my ass. He grabbed my hair and pulled my head back, and I gave out a loud moan. I felt his breath on my neck as he continued to drive against me in a controlled manner; meanwhile, some of his fingers slide into my mouth that was already open because I was panting uncontrollably. He wet his fingers with my spit and then sneaked through my shirt with his wet fingers to massage my nipples with it.

"Your nipples are really hard, you slut," he panted in my ear while I feel his other hand close my throat.

Yes, squeeze my throat, but I thought, treat me like your slut. I enjoyed the moment he shut off my windpipe, and I totally surrendered to him, and I wish he would dominate me. As I started to shake my legs because of the lack of air, it seemed as if he could read my mind. He turned my head around so that I stood with my back to the front door, with my face toward him. I saw his face and another horny shock hit my whole body; his hair was messed up, it was finally not so smoothly combed back with a heap of hair spray and gel in it, it was wild and hung in front of his face, and his expression was also wild, to say the least. As if some sort of primordial instinct drove him to dominate me.

With that dirty horny look from him, he looked at me, I am completely stuck in his look, and suddenly he pulls his arm back and raises his hand in the air. I look at his hand and see how it is at full speed on my face goes off. Jordan hits me full in the face, and I hear myself scream softly, my eyes start to tear with the blow. This is exactly what I want; he knows this, we have fantasized about this together before. The raw look on his face remains, he hits me in the mouth again and again and again. Every time with full power, I love that he dares and trust that I can handle it. I feel the tears slowly leaving my eyes, and in the meantime, my pussy fluid also runs down my thighs. I keep looking at Jordan and see his dirty look soften, a sweet little smile appears on his lips, and he slowly presses against me again. He grabs my face and rubs his fingers gently over the spot where his handprint is still burning, he kisses me sweetly, but soon we end up in passionate kisses again. We almost crawled into each other. We were so entangled. I went wild with my fingers through his hair and put my legs around him. He drove me up against the door as we continued to kiss each other, our tongues following each other as if they had never done anything else, and we moaned as if we were actually fucking each other. But we didn't. Moreover, we had never even seen each other naked in real life.

I had no idea how long we had been standing against that front door, but at a certain moment, we stood against each other, gasping straight in each other's face while we looked at each other without saying anything, but the energy that flowed between us caused no words to be needed. Suddenly he pulled up my shirt and bra. I stood there; with ruined mascara, my hair so messed up that it could have been a bird's nest, red cheeks from the blows they had caught, with my big tits exposed to his eyes in only my leggings at half-past ten. Jordan took a few steps back while I'm still panting at the front door. He looked at me from head to toe, and when I saw my breasts, a naughty smile appeared on his face.

"Well satisfied?" I said, thinking of how I had planned to keep my tits on board.

"They're great," he replied as he reached out and groped me like some kind of predator. I smile shyly and stick my chest out to give him all the access he wanted. Jordan pushed his hard cock between my thighs, making me feel his shaft against my clit as he pulled and shook my tits, fingering my nipples and grunting in frustration. He unzipped his pants, his cock springing out and the wetness of his precum now staining my leggings.

"You'll do as I say," he commanded, turning me around and pulling me back into him. I felt him push me down, so my face was on the ground, but my hips and ass were in the air. Jordan peeled back my leggings, slapping my ass when he saw I wasn't wearing any panties. The next thing I felt was the cool wetness of his cock slide up and down my ass cheeks. I tried to spread my ass for him, but he just laughed.

"No, I want to spear you myself," he said, pushing my arms out the way. He leaned back, and I felt the tip of his cock being pressed against my clit, the juices from my pussy coating his dick. Suddenly, I felt the tip at the entrance of my asshole, pushing hard and fast inside of me, making me moan and gasp.

"Take it," he groaned as he pushed until I could feel his full, heavy balls squish against my ass.

"There it is," he moaned, and I was surprised to feel him cumming into my ass.

"So soon?" I asked, slightly annoyed that I had got nothing. He just laughed and slapped my ass as he pulled out.

"Yeah, that's what sluts get, used," he

replied, jerking his cock over my back and finishing his load. Jordan pulled his pants back on and kissed me on the head before walking out the door.

I raced to my phone and messaged him immediately.

That was amazing. Thank you so much for fulfilling that fantasy of mine! I wrote.

I loved it too. I felt so bad for leaving like that, are you ok? He replied only moments later.

Yeah, it was great. See you next week at yours, I answered before going into the shower after one of our many fantasies had finally played out.

Delicious First Time

It is 8:30 am, as agreed I ring exactly at this time. We have until 11:45 am, not really long, but I guess it has to be enough for a first session. I see your head look around the corner of the window, and a moment later, I see the door open. For the neighbors, I will be someone who comes to sell something. Looking good in a suit and suitcase with me. What they cannot see is that, as agreed, you are only wearing a bathrobe. I am standing in front of the door, and it is not open further than it is necessary to let me in. I walk inside and immediately close the front door, so our first step has been taken. You let me come in further by keeping the door to the room open, I see in a flash that you are more beautiful than I expected. I take a seat on the couch and see that you have poured the coffee in accordance with the agreement, so that means two things, you have paid close attention to the clock because I see that the coffee is still steaming and you knew that I was going to be here at exactly 8:30.

I take my first sip of coffee and then say very quietly, "get undressed." Your eyes give you away as they sparkle with excitement and pretend innocence. Your body has already responded, and the bathrobe is already on the floor. Knowing that nakedness makes you both shy and horny, I will let you stand for a while. You have your arms tight along your body, and your head is tilted as it should be, slightly bent down and you look at the floor. After a few minutes I get up, I see your body tighten; here stands the woman who wants to be used so disrespectfully with a lot of respect. The lady who wants to be a whore and protected at the same time, who would like to be used as a lady for the outside world but as a slut and a lust object behind closed doors. The woman who is not keen on pain, but wants to be dealt with harshly in the right mood and sometimes wants to be punished. Would it now become a reality after years and years of fantasy?

I walk around you, and I let my hand go over your ass and feel that your buttocks pull together, and a shudder passes through your body. I see that your nipples have hardened spontaneously, your body has betrayed itself and tells me that it is almost ready. Then I stroke your belly, your breasts and the rest of your body, calm and soft, but then you suddenly feel how I squeeze your hard nipple. You can't think long about it because at the same time you hear me ask, is the alarm clock at 11:15 am. With a nod, you confirm that the alarm clock is set to sound at that time. I stand in front of you, press my hand under your chin so that you have to look at me and I kiss you. First carefully, but it won't be long before our tongues are in an exciting fight with each other. I stop abruptly, you keep your eyes closed and you hear me say, look at me. You immediately open your eyes and I give you a short but clear assignment.

"Suck me," I demand. You seem to sink

straight through your knees without thinking, and you impatiently open my pants and lower them. I get out of my pants and I feel that you are fully engaged with your assignment, you alternately lick my balls and jerk my stiffening cock. Then you take my hard pole in your mouth and start to suck me deeply. I take your head between my hands; that way, I keep your head in place and I start to move my hips back and forth. I am not going to let you blow now, but I am fucking your mouth, sometimes quietly, then louder. Your lips enclose my big hard pole and I am enjoying myself, using you for my pleasure. Then I let go of your head and see that you diligently try to get my cock deeper down your throat than I did when I fucked you. And with pride, I see that you can almost get my monster balls deep down your throat. But after 10-15 minutes I feel that I'm going to be ready in a minute and I don't want to do that yet. A short, "stand up" is enough to make you stand. You are standing in front of me; I see that your lips are wet and your eyes show that you did not mind. In my direction, you lean forward and spread your legs and stand bent over with your hands supported on the coffee table, waiting for what is to come. I'm going to stand behind you and without any reservations, I push my ass behind your pussy lips. They are so wet that I can suddenly push through deeply; apparently, you have become very horny from having to blow and get fucked in your mouth because you are soaking wet and I do not only feel that you are wet, I hear your pussy when I'm fucking you deeply. While fucking, I play with your overhanging tits and I don't have to wait long for your nipples to be very hard again. Apparently, your nipples are very sensitive, I take them between my fingers and while fucking, I start working your nipples harder and harder. I am enjoying myself to the full, but to my horror, I feel that you are almost done; that is a shame I would have liked to have used you a little longer this way. But I don't want you to cum just yet. So I stop abruptly and instruct you to lick my dick clean, something you apparently like to do. I immediately punish your attempt to blow me by a short, "leave that," I do not need to explain to you further what I mean because you stop immediately. Then I say okay and you get up. My "walk-up" brings you in doubt again; you see that I immediately pack my suitcase to take it upstairs and your doubt comes up again for a moment. But apparently, you feel that you can trust me because you walk up ahead full of conviction. You know that you can use two words at all times, pause and stop are sacred and no further explanation is needed. At the top I see that you have indeed put the blindfold on the pillow, next to it is a dildo, I do not know how many you have, but I do know that this is your favorite. Again it appears that "blindfold" is sufficient to make it clear what I want. That makes me feel good. You walk to the headboard and put on the blindfold, the fully convincing manner in which you do that shows that the question of whether you have faith in me is now answered. I leave you lying on your back on the bed and I gently instruct you to make yourself horny like you do when no one is there. I sit down quietly and see how you are going to caress your breasts with your hands and your nipples react immediately again. So I let you play for a while, I see that you are now rubbing a hand over your pussy and I grab the dildo and put it on your stomach. You do not respond immediately, but just continue to caress your breast and your pussy. Moments later your other hand goes to your pussy and you open your pussy with one hand, with the other hand you caress the inside of your pussy lips that glisten with your juices.

I hear you moaning, and I see that you know I am totally relaxed and you want to share this intimate moment with me. Your finger is now playing a game with your clit. Then I hear you ask, may I please treat myself as a whore in your presence? I barely said yes, and you grab the dildo, and without waiting, you push it completely into your pussy in one go. Apparently, you knew that your pussy was wet enough to receive it in this way, a deep sigh passes through you, it is clearly visible a familiar feeling. So you have a clear difference between simply spoiling yourself and permitting yourself to be a whore. Because the quietly self-stroking woman is now a horny whore, who pulls her legs up and is fucking herself hard and deep, it is clear that you enjoy this and I see and feel how you are getting hornier and hornier, you pull alternately hard on your nipples, while the other hand pumps the dildo into and out of your pussy. This is really a very beautiful sight. I see that you are about to come and give the instruction.

"You can't come." You startle, and your movements become calmer, your breath is howling through your throat. Then I grab a pillow and place it under you, your pussy will raise, and you will grab the dildo with your two hands that you move back and forth between your pussy lips. Then you put the dildo in front of your butt. I see that this is going to be tough, but you will continue; you let the dildo rest halfway and I see you come to rest. Your ass is clearly not used to so much; apparently, you have just discovered how much you enjoy this. Then you begin to move the dildo very gently back and forth, first 1 cm but a little later 2 cm then 3 cm back and forth and a little later, you pump the dildo back and forth — almost all the way out then around half in again. Now you only move the dildo with one hand, the other looks for your nipples. They are not treated very gently by you; I see that you pull them very hard. You ask me, can I please come in just a moment? I think you deserve it for a while and say okay, as you continue to fuck yourself like a whore. You stop playing with your nipples abruptly and your hand goes to your clit. With a finger, you massage your clit. You know your body well because you have immediately found the right pace. The dildo still goes back and forth at the same pace; it seems that your hand is on autopilot. Your movements remain in the same rhythm for a moment, but then I see that you let your finger pass over your clit very quickly and I see that the dildo, until now, has been halfway in your ass. I see your body come vibrating, the moisture runs out of your pussy, and your whole body is shaking

Then I quickly grab the dildo and pull it out of your ass, and at the same time, I say stop. You are shocked; having to stop in the middle of your orgasm is not really easy. I lie down next to you and instruct you to remove the blindfold to sit on my face. I see that I have confused you by what I said, and so instruct you to open your pussy and position yourself on my tongue. The tingling of the half-broken orgasm is still in your body, and the moment your pussy touches my tongue, I feel that your body is continuing with what it was doing. You don't care anymore, you rub your pussy over my tongue and now your cunt only wants one thing. Your knees cling around me and you fuck yourself on my tongue, I have to swallow because your cunt juices pour out of you. I keep licking and swallowing and enjoy to the fullest when I feel that you are almost at the end of your orgasm, I grab your nipples and I work them hard. Your diminishing orgasm increases again and you look at me confused, your body was used to having finished, but due to the unexpected processing of your nipples, it flares up further. Your orgasm is long, your body is in a haze, I let go of your nipples, grab your ass and so you press on my mouth and feel the last trembling of your orgasm on my lips and tongue. I look up and see a tear in your eyes, that's probably not because you don't like it. Then your orgasm decreases and you have your body under control again. At least you think so.

I turn around and get away from you; you lie down on your back to recover from your orgasm. Too bad for you because I quickly grab the rope that lies next to the bed. Before you know what's going on, I have tied your right hand to the bed, and a little later, your left hand is also tied. You want to raise your head, but I press it back into the pillow, I grab the blindfold and put it in front of your eyes. You now leave your head resting and waiting for what is to come; you don't have to wait long for that. After I quickly tied both your feet, you know

I'm going to use your body now, a long-fulfilled wish comes true, to be used like a slut, whore, lust object by the orgasm you've just had, you're really in for it in the mood.

I lie down on you and effortlessly push my big hard pole into your cunt, now it's my cunt, my property and I do whatever I want with it, and I'll tell you that too. After I quietly fucked you for a while with long and deep strokes, I enjoy your body by fucking you harder and harder. I see that you are enjoying it, and I squeeze you briefly but hard. You are shocked and the intoxication of pleasure has been broken; you are again aware of the fact that you are now being used as a pleasure object and immediately, the intoxication of horniness is back. However, I feel that if I continue, I will come so easily and I do not want that. So I get rid of you, the sigh you make tells me everything, that you wouldn't have minded if I had fucked myself in you right now, but that's not what I want now.

I'm going to fuck your ass now, but because I am so big, I have to train your ass to take me. So I grab the suitcase and take out the ball rod. I first wet it by pulling it back and forth a few times in your pussy; I immediately feel that you do not know what the ball rod is, but that this will certainly soon be your favorite. The best dildo cannot compete with the intense pleasure of the balls. Now that the rod is wet enough, I press it against your butt, and the first three balls simply go into your butt, the 4th also just goes so I stop. I leave the bar and grab your own dildo and push it into your pussy. Then I tease you by moving the two back and forth; I see that you do not know how to take this and thrash from side to side on the bed in pleasure. I decide that I'll make you cum one more time again. I don't have to put a lot of effort into it; I gently move the dildo and the balls of the rod back and forth and look at your body to see the language of your body when you are cumming. And I don't have to wait long for that; your nipples swell, your breath goes faster, then you hear me say you are my horny whore, my slut and yes my new private whore is coming again. I now feel that your ass is also ready to receive the next ball, and I push the rod a bit deeper and a scream of pleasure fills the room. I pull the dildo out of your cunt and let you get ready on the rod in your ass. Your body contracts again when I pull the rod out and you fall back on the bed — totally drowsy with orgasm.

I loosen the ropes of your feet and press your legs up; I grab the pillow and press it under your buttocks so that your cunt and ass come up well. Then I whisper in your ear, "whore, I'm going to deflower your ass" your fright reaction doesn't come, and you scream, "yes, I've never been fucked there." Now I don't wait anymore, I take a position and press my cock against your ass. I see that your body is pretty relaxed, and you have the confidence that I will stop if you use one of the words. I also see that your ass hurts when I go deeper and deeper into you, but you don't think about saying stop or pause, I only hear yes yes yes. Then I am completely in you, I wait a moment and I hear a deep sigh coming out of your mouth, because of the horniness in your body you are now able to receive me. Now I start pumping slowly and feel that I have become very horny because of all this. I start pumping harder and harder and I know that I am now deflowering a woman who has had this wish for years. Apparently, the wish is so great that the pain does not touch her. You ask, "may I please come again," I know you have wanted to be taken anally for so long and I also want to come. So I tell you what a whore and slut I think you are, I feel how your ass squeezes together while you come and that is too much. I can no longer stay calm. I come deep in your ass and I start spraying and feel that we are both cumming hard. I stay in your butt for a while; in the meantime, I will loosen your hands and take off your blindfold. Your face shines from ear to ear. I say nothing; I pull out of you and turn on your stomach. Then I pick up a whip from my suitcase that I know is suitable for someone who is not used to whip. I only decide to work your butt with the whip and let the whip do its work on your butt. After a while, I think it is enough for a first introduction to the whip and briefly, but forcefully, I say, go to the shower. You jump up and walk to the shower; everything shows you have no shame for me.

The tap opens, and when the water has the right temperature, we step under it together. I soap you and wash your body from head to toe; now, there is no place that I don't know. I also note that you have a beautiful body, not many women your age have such a beautiful body. I do feel that I am getting horny again; the radiance of your body has a strong effect on me. I see you looking, and I tell you that I find you so very attractive, your eyes speak volumes. Knowing that you are not used to sucking a man until the end, I immediately know what I will do with you. I turn off the tap; we dry ourselves and go back to the bedroom. I lie down on the bed, and a short, "get me hard" is enough to get you back to work. You go to work, your tongue works my pole and my balls and you start to suck me deeply. I let it come over me and relax for a while, startled by the alarm, we know we have to stop; the school will be out in 30 minutes. But first I lay you flat on the bed, I come up and start to fuck between your tits, you lick every time I come forward between your tits that you have pressed hard against my rod. I see you nodding, without saying anything we both know what you want to say to me. I feel that I am going to cum and I start to fuck your mouth, not long after that, I feel my cock squirt into your mouth. Keeping a close eye on your face, I see that I don't have to stop but can continue quietly. You swallow and swallow and pride radiates from your face; it is really clear, you are really proud to be used for the first time in your life as a whore.

Submissive Wife

Evan was home earlier than his wife, which was unusual. They both lived and worked in the same city but had enormously different hours. Evan has earned enough money for him and Alyssa to live comfortably for the rest of their lives, but Alyssa insisted on working, even if it was just a few days a week.

Evan went to his man cave to do some work on the motor he had been building when he remembered that he had told Alyssa he would fix her laptop. He picked it up and turned it on. The screen glowed and was then dimmed. He lifted the search bar and surprised his eyes. The search history was filled with extensive searches of BDSM scenes. He gave into the curiosity that arose in him, leafed through the bookmark history and clicked on the first website that came up. It was the link to a site that focused on humiliation, beating, and submission.

The other bookmarks led him to stories of submission of women submitting to their husbands and in their urge to contact dominant and dominant strangers who broke in and forced the woman to obey them. Evan was shocked, but the more he immersed himself in his wife's browsing history, the more intrigued he was.

He and Alyssa had been married for almost ten years; they were in their forties. Sex hadn't been exciting for a while. He had not complained because there was no reason for it; it was a stable love affair. They had grown together comfortably, which was to be expected. Looking through the links, he began to wonder how many of his wife's hidden desires could be realized. Evan felt his cock shake with the idea that his wife should obey his word. He got a kick when he looked at things that were taboo. He slowly went through her browsing history and watched every scene with growing lust. The knock of the door brought him back to reality. Alyssa was back, and Evan couldn't shake the thought that their relationship was about to change. He couldn't tell whether it would get better or worse or that this might be the beginning of the end.

The conversation during dinner was light. Evan was distracted during most of the meal, and Alyssa noticed.

"Is everything all right, dear? Is everything okay at work?" Asked Alyssa, who was playing with her food. It was one of the few times that she had come home after Evan and that something seemed to have happened to him. She noticed it the moment she opened the door.

Work is going great; that's not what distracts me. He kept thinking. He had thought of her secret obsession. He had never rated Alyssa as the type of woman triggered by BDSM. But that very fact had quite excited him. He could not stop his imagination about how this would work in practice. He had to know.

"Alyssa, I want you to be honest with me, I

was trying to fix your laptop, and I found some things," he paused and gave her time to understand what he was trying to say.

"You... Oh... Eh... That's just... I wasn't... Uh..." She seemed helpless and looked everywhere except where he sat. She was clearly ashamed.

"Alyssa, I'm fine, really, I just didn't know you'd be interested in things like that. Is that what you are? A submissive girl?" Evan asked softly, stroking her hands on the table.

"Yes, I mean, I think so, I happened upon a BDSM by accident, and since then, it's all I can think of. It has taken possession of my whole mind. I want to serve you and obey you. I don't really know much about it, but I've been researching online. It is something that I want to try with you as my dominant and I hope you don't love me less, of course, it's okay if you don't do it..." She started.

"I'll do it, and I am intrigued by the idea, the truth is that all the time you are talking about it my cock is rock hard, I have resisted the urge to bend you over the table and fuck you," Evan admitted. Alyssa stared at him with big, voluptuous eyes.

"What's stopping you? Do you want to become my dominant tonight? Alyssa asked. They did not often have quickies. Her pussy got wet at the thought. She was already wet and horny.

"I do. I want to be your dominant." He said. His cock hardened painfully in his pants.

"Does my master still want to fuck me over the table?" Alyssa lowered her gaze and asked in a soft, soft tone. Evan moaned when he saw her gaze.

"Stand up! Bend over the table and lift your skirt," he ordered, still not sure if Alyssa would meet his requirement. She stood up and lifted her skirt over her ass. Her panties were already steeped in the thought of Evan, who had her under control. He wanted to take it easy, but the look of his wife's pussy, so wet and the needy noises that Alyssa made went straight to his cock. He grabbed the thin fabric of her panties and pulled them aside. Her pussy was on fire. She burned with a desire to be filled. Evan smiled and stuck his fat veined cock into Alyssa's pussy. She screamed, but it was pure pleasure. Evan grabbed her fists that were anchored on her hips and pulled her arms back so that the hard blows of his cock dived deeper into her. She moaned, begging him.

"Harder, Oh god, please fuck me harder, Master," she screamed while her pussy was gushing. Evan growled and fucked her harder. He had never fucked her so raw and animal-like. The harder he fucked in her, the more his cock grew in size. He exploded, squirting streaks of his seed deep into her pussy. Alyssa shivered and screamed, the pleasure drove her to cumming as fast as his cock did. She moaned and screamed until her pussy exploded around his exploding cock.

"Oh, tonight has only just started," Even said as he positioned Alyssa with one leg on the table and filled her with his cock once again.

Evan had started an online investigation. He visited various BDSM websites, so he learned more about the art of being dominant. He found a website that appealed to him. Through an online advertisement, he came to the website of Mistress Isabella. The website was nicely set up and laid out with clear and playful explanations about all BDSM concepts. It was good to get such a clear explanation. What triggered him, even more, was the webpage about BDSM workshops. Mistress Isabella works from an SM Studio in the same city specializing in BDSM. In fact, it couldn't have been more perfect. A professional Mistress could tell him everything about all the aspects of BDSM and show him how a Master acts towards his slave girl. Evan made an appointment with Mistress Isabella.

From the search history of his wife, he knew that she found videos about humiliation and power exchange exciting. He wanted their first experience as a master and slave to become even more memorable than those on the dining table.

Evan walked to the SM studio from his studio, not sure what to expect. What he saw was actually just a terraced house. At least it seemed that way. The workshop had to be a one-to-one experience. As soon as he came in, a secretary was waiting for him at the door or at least he assumed it was a secretary. She smiled.

"Good morning, please follow me." She waited until he was completely inside before quickly leading him through a number of corridors to a room. Evan held his breath and hardly made any noise. If there was such a thing as a sex church, this was it. Mistress Isabella sat behind a huge desk, all brown wood with leather aspects. She was dressed in black latex from head to toe. Her lips were deep red lipstick, and her hair was tucked into a tight bun. The angles of her face were sharp, rounded off with full lips.

"Welcome, sit." She said sharply, wasting no time on courtesies.

"Thank you, Mistress Isabella; it is a pleasure." Evan sat and waited.

"So, from our conversation on the phone, you want to be a Dom?" She asked.

"I do want to become a Dom; it is something that my wife and I are interested in. I think she is more interested in mind play and humiliation. The truth is that I know very little about it. Except for what I have viewed online." Evan said.

"Mindplay is simple," said Mistress Isabella. "Because your sub is also your wife, you have a head start on BDSM people who have just met. I do not have to ask if this is a relationship for a limited period of time. It is, first and foremost, your duty to take care of your sub. Because this is not a relationship based solely on sexual satisfaction, it is the most important thing you have," stated Mistress Isabella. Evan nodded. It was easy enough. He loved his wife more than anything else in the world.

"Good, you will discuss boundaries, both hard and soft, know each other's boundaries, understand each other, and establish trust. Most of it is halfway considering the nature of your relationship, but it is very different in the Dom / Sub relationship. Training and understanding of each other, you will not only have to know how to act while playing but also in the overall relationship." She went on to explain.

"Okay, I understand it so far." He said. "Now, about the reason that you are here. Mindplay is not as mainstream as some other kinks, but it can be just as fun if limits are set. Mindplay is changing the perception of the submissive partner's reality, credible depiction, or sensory deprivation in a credible way. You said that your wife has fantasies about a masked Dom who breaks into your house and forces her submission?" Mistress Isabella asked.

"Yes, I realized that she watched multiple videos of those in that category."

"That could be a good starting point until you get all the tools needed for more complex scenes. Now on to humiliation. Victoria, come here." Mistress Isabella spoke through the intercom on her desk.

"Yes, Mistress." A trusted female voice answered. The woman who had shown him the office walked in earlier.

"Evan, this is my sub-Victoria, Victoria greet the gentleman." Commanded Mistress Isabella.

"Good morning sir, it's a pleasure meeting you." Victoria nodded her head. Evan stared at the woman. Her politeness, her respective attitude, it was almost the way his wife had begged him the last night to fuck her, only more.

"Victoria, remove your clothes." Mistress Isabella spoke. Victoria stared at the floor and moved uncomfortably back and forth. Slowly her hands reluctantly to the shirt she was wearing and began loosening the buttons. Her cheeks were colored. It was clear that she was embarrassed. The blush led to her full round tits that she exposed. She undressed slowly until she wore nothing.

"Dear girl, stand by the window until I tell you something else." Mistress Isabella pointed out.

Victoria looked like she was going to faint, she shuffled uncomfortably on her feet until she stood by the window.

"Humiliation can work in different ways or in different situations; it's easier if you know the person's trigger. Victoria, my pet, is painfully shy and would never have taken off her clothes for a stranger, nor would she have stood completely naked in front of the window. You can tell by the blush that is so visible on her wonderful skin, no matter how embarrassed she is. But I know that if I caress her tight pussy now, she would be incredibly wet, you see she gets a kick from the embarrassment she feels, and it turns her to be so malleable to my desires, she doesn't have to like it, but my wish will always be her assignment. Will your wife respond in the same way?" Mistress asked, looking at Victoria as if she were hungry.

"I'm sure she would." Evan smiled. He knew for sure. His wife was in for a treat.

Alyssa slid into bed when a warm hand clenched around her mouth. A hard body fell on her, holding her in place despite her struggle.

"Don't shout, if you do that, I may be forced to punish you." A loud male voice whispered. Alyssa swallowed, relaxing her body as soon as she felt the hard length of the man's erection.

"Dear girl, you are a good little slave, aren't you?" He whispered as he rocked his hips against her soft ass. He already knew what he intended to do with her. Alyssa whined. Her hips rocked with their own thoughts.

"Strip, I want to see you naked." He ordered her to lean on the bed and give her the space to stand on her feet. Alyssa stood on shaky feet. Her hands were shaking as she looked at the masked man lying on the bed. He looked angry and held a whip in his hands.

"You little slut, you don't wear anything to sleep in when your husband isn't home? You ask to be fucked, don't you?" He asked. Alyssa bit her lip, fear mixed in her pussy, making her wet. She moaned. Crack! The whip almost painfully hit her skin.

"Answer me, slave!"

"Yes, master!" She shouted.

"Dance for me, slowly, sexy." He whispered. His eyes shot down to hide the flame in his eyes as he looked at her. Alyssa moaned and rocked her hips for fear of a new lash. The masked man loosened his pants and stroked his liberated throbbing dick at Alyssa's sight. She slowly turned her hips and rocked like she was fucking an invisible dick. Her nipples peaked and hardened. A trail of wet, hot pussy nectar slid down her thighs. He turned his hands around his cock, enjoying watching her. He wanted to fuck her hard, wanted her to scream.

"Crawl over to me, little girl." He commanded. Alyssa did as she was told, too far into the fantasy to worry. She crawled until she was on the edge of the bed. He released his cock. Alyssa lay on the bed and felt the warmth of his body. Without warning, he whipped the whip across her sensitive, swollen nipples.

"Ah! Master! "She screamed. He didn't relent. The lashes of the whip went lower and lower until he was thrashing against the sensitive head of her clit! She screamed, wriggling her hips. The lashes didn't hurt; they made her crazy. He held her with one hand and hit her with the other. The blows fell on her pussy and pushed the mind-expanding pleasure she already had higher and higher.

"Fuuuuck master!" Alyssa screamed when she came. The man did not wait; he dragged her by her hips, pounded his dick into her cunt. Alyssa screamed again. Her orgasm did not stop; instead, it interfered with another and another.

"Who is the owner of this pussy?" The man growled, he banged at her with hard blows. His cock was already ready to explode.

"You Master, you!" Alyssa shouted as a new orgasm raged through her.

"Fuck, yes!" He hissed with pleasure that ran through him and exploded out of his cock into long, hot streams of seed. A few minutes passed when he pulled out of her and dragged her close. Her hands touched his unmasked face with a look of pure love.

"You own me, Master," Alyssa said with a smile. Evan smiled and kissed her gently.